The Frog Prince

Miles Kelly

Once, there lived a princess called Molly, who lived in a grand castle.

Every day, Princess Molly walked into the woods to play catch with her golden ball.

Her favourite spot was near a well.

One day, Molly was playing catch as usual. But she missed the ball and it bounced into the well with a splash.

The princess peered into the well and wailed. "Don't upset yourself," said a **croaky voice**. "I can get your ball back."

Then a frog jumped onto the edge of the well. "Really?" Molly asked. "Yes," replied the frog. "But what will you give me, if I do?"

"Oh, anything," said Molly. "Then promise that we will be best friends, and let me eat from your golden plate, and sleep on your pillow," said the frog.

"Yes, yes," agreed the princess. "I promise."

So the frog **jumped** into the well. After a minute or two, he reappeared with the ball. The princess was thrilled!

She scooped it up and
raced home.

"Wait!" called the frog. "Pick me up!
I cannot go as fast as you!" But
Molly had forgotten
all about her helper.

That evening, when Molly was eating dinner, there came a
splish, splash, splish, splash along the hallway.

Then there was a knock at the door and a voice cried,

"Princess, let me in!"

Molly opened the door to see the frog. He jumped into her arms.

The king asked,
"Who is it Molly?"
"It's a horrid frog," she said,
and explained what had
happened at the well that day.

"Princess, remember
your promise!"
croaked the frog.

The king said, "You must
keep your promise, Molly."
So she helped the frog onto
the table, then glared at him.

Once the frog was on the table he said, "Now push your plate nearer so we can eat together." Molly did as he asked.

The frog munched his way through three courses while Molly barely ate a thing. At last the frog was full.

"Delicious!"

The frog yawned. "I'm tired, please put me to bed." Molly scowled, but carried him upstairs. The frog hopped up to her bedside, croaking, "Let me sleep on your pillow."

The princess groaned, but let the frog leap onto the pillow. And there he slept until the light of day, when he hopped down and out of the palace.

"Zzzzz!"

The same thing happened the following day, and the princess had to let the frog eat from her plate and sleep on her pillow. Again he left when dawn broke.

On the third day, the princess looked forward to seeing the frog. His jokes made her laugh. Once again he slept on the princess's pillow.

When Molly awoke the next morning, she saw a prince with kind eyes standing beside her bed. "Who are you?" asked Molly.

The prince said how a witch had enchanted him to be a frog. Molly broke the spell by keeping her promise.

"You do still look a bit like a frog!" she said.

Molly and Prince Toby became best friends. They saw each other a lot. Their favourite game was basketball, using the golden ball of course.

Then one day, when they were grown-up, Toby asked Molly to **marry** him. Of course she said yes.

After the wedding, they set off for Toby's kingdom in a golden carriage, with crowds cheering along the way. They lived happily ever after.

Hooray!

The End

My Fairytale Time

The Frog Prince

Time to read! Little ones will love the bright illustrations on every page of this beautiful picture book. The story has been simply retold in a clear and engaging way to encourage reading.

ISBN 978-1-78617-427-7

Copyright © 2018 Miles Kelly Publishing Ltd
Harding's Barn, Bardfield End Green, Thaxted,
Essex, CM6 3PX, UK. All rights reserved

Printed in China, Jul 2019, FAF119

UK £5.99/US $7.95

www.mileskelly.net

Little Teddy
Left Behind

Anne Mangan

Joanne Moss

A Soft-to-Touch Book

Little Tiger Press